Common Core Lessons & Activities:
Habitats

By Carole Marsh
Published by Gallopade International, Inc.

Printed in the U.S.A. (Peachtree City, Georgia)

TABLE OF CONTENTS

G: Includes Graphic Organizer
GO: Graphic Organizer is also available 8½" x 11" online
download at www.gallopade.com/client/g
(numbers above correspond to the graphic organi

I0892143

What Is a Habitat?

Read the text and answer the questions.

A habitat is the environment where an animal, plant, or other type of organism naturally lives. Just like your home is where you live, a habitat is an organisms' home!

A habitat is a home, but it is much more than *just* a home. A habitat contains the food, water, and shelter that an organism needs to survive. It includes physical features such as soil, moisture, temperature, and sunlight, as well as the availability of food and the presence of predators.

Organisms naturally live in habitats where they are able to meet their needs. For example, animals live in habitats where they can find food to eat, water to drink, shelter for protection, and where they are suited to the climate. Plants live where they get the right temperature, amount of sunlight, nutrients from the soil, and moisture. An organism such as bacteria lives where the temperature, moisture, and nutrients meet its needs, too.

Habitats come in all shapes and sizes. An ant's habitat may be an anthill and a small surrounding area where it gets food and water. In contrast, a cheetah's habitat may be a vast area of African grassland that covers hundreds of miles where it roams and hunts. A habitat for a micro-organism might be the body of its host.

1. Match each of the following questions to whether they are best answered by paragraph 1, 2, 3, or 4 of the text. Then use the text to answer each question.
   A. What features does a habitat include?
   B. How big is a habitat?
   C. Why do organisms live in certain habitats?
   D. What is the definition of habitat?

2. *A simile is a comparison using the word "like" or "as."*
   A. What simile is used in the text to describe a habitat?
   B. What is the author's purpose for using the simile?
   C. Is it effective? Why or why not?

3. Choose an animal you are familiar with and describe its habitat. Use the text as a guide of what information to include in your description.

Meeting Basic Needs

Read the text and answer the questions.

Organisms meet their basic needs in their habitats. For plants, these basic needs include sunlight, water, and nutrients. For animals, these basic needs include food, water, and shelter.

Plants and animals must live in a suitable habitat in order to meet their basic needs for survival. For example, a plant that needs a lot of sunlight and water, such as a sunflower, lives best in a sunny field. Similarly, an animal that has legs for walking and lungs for breathing, such as a horse or elephant, lives best on land. The Giant Panda eats almost 40 pounds of bamboo daily! It only lives in the bamboo forests of China because it would struggle to find enough food if it lived anywhere else.

Plants and animals sometimes have special characteristics that help them meet their basic needs for survival. These characteristics make it easier for them to find food, water, or shelter in their habitat. For example, a camel stores water in a special hump on its back, allowing it to survive in its hot, dry desert habitat. The striped coat of a Bengal Tiger allows it to hide in tall grasses, giving it protection from predators and allowing it to sneak up on its prey.

1. What is the relationship between an organism and its habitat?
2. A. Is a cave a suitable habitat for a sunflower? Why or why not?
   B. Is the ocean a suitable habitat for a horse? Why or why not?
3. A. How is a camel suited to its desert habitat?
   B. What can you infer about plants that live in a desert habitat?
4. Explain how each of the words defined describes a purpose of a Bengal Tiger's stripes.
   A. deceive: to cause someone to believe something untrue
   B. camouflage: to hide or disguise by use of shape or coloring
   C. imitate: to follow or copy a style or way of doing something
5. *Large areas of China's bamboo forests have been cut down.*
   A. List three effects this has likely had on Giant Pandas.
   B. Predict three additional consequences if it continues.

Animal Behaviors

Read the text and answer the questions.

Animals live in a habitat where they can meet their basic needs. However, basic needs don't usually just "show up." Usually, animals must work very hard in order to survive. As a result, many animals have developed specific behaviors to help. These behavior adaptations can help them meet their basic needs, and they can give them an advantage over predators or prey in their habitat. Behavior adaptations usually develop over a very long period of time—usually over many generations. However, the more intelligent an animal is, the quicker it is able to adapt its behavior.

One way some animals adapt their behavior is by working as part of a group. For example, ants work as a group, called a colony, to gather food and build a home. Wolves hunt as a group, called a pack, to surround and catch their prey. Buffalo travel in groups, called herds, to protect themselves from predators.

Another way some animals adapt their behavior is by migrating. Migration is the movement of an animal from one habitat to another. For example, geese cannot survive in the cold, so when winter approaches, they fly to a warmer habitat. When Grey Whales are ready to give birth, they migrate from the cold Arctic Ocean to warm water off the coast of Mexico. Animals may also migrate in search of food, water, or shelter.

Many animals adapt their behavior by using resources in their habitats to build shelters. For example, polar bears dig ice dens in the snow. Mice and moles dig burrows in the ground. And, beavers build lodges made from sticks and tree branches.

Hibernation is another way that animals adapt their behavior. In cold climates, some mammals hibernate, or take a "long nap," during the coldest months. Most bears eat a lot during the fall to build up body fat. Then, when winter arrives, they crawl into a cave and sleep for several months. While they hibernate, their body functions slow down so they use much less energy than if they were active, and they rely on their extra fat for energy while they sleep.

Other animal behavior adaptations include "sunning" to warm body temperature and "playing dead" to avoid predators.

1. Define <u>behaviors</u> as it is used in the text.
2. Why do animals adapt their behaviors?
3. To complete the table, list five animal behaviors and explain how each behavior helps animals with that adaptation to survive in their habitat.

Behavior	How Helps With Survival

4. *Humans adapt their behavior to their habitat too.*
For each scenario, name the type of behavior adaptation demonstrated and explain its purpose:

A. *Native American tribes in the Great Plains region of the U.S. used to move their camp from place to place in search of buffalo.*

B. *In the mid to late 1800s, pioneers who traveled to the Midwest often built homes out of sod "bricks" because there were no trees to cut to build the traditional wooden houses they were used to.*

C. *Many Canadians have Florida vacation homes they go to during the winter.*

D. *When you have a fever, it's usually good to stay home and get lots of rest so your body can fight off germs and get well.*

E. *You are part of a community.*

Writing Prompt: Imagine you have left Europe to be one of the first colonists to come to America. Use what you know about colonial American history, and what you read about animal behavior adaptations in the text, to write a first-person narrative describing your new "habitat" and at least three ways you might adapt your behavior based on your new habitat.

Structural Adaptations

Read the text and complete Parts A, B, and C.

Animals survive in "harsh" habitats all around the world. For example, a polar bear stays warm in freezing arctic weather, a snake finds food in a scorching desert, and a deep sea fish survives in the dark on the sunless ocean floor. How do animals survive in such varied habitats? Over long periods of time, animals have developed special characteristics, called structural adaptations, that help them find food, water, and shelter in the unique habitats where they live.

PART A: Read each text and identify at least three structural adaptations. Then explain how each adaptation helps the animal survive in its habitat.

"I don't have legs like most animals, but that's just fine. A horse's hooves or a human's skinny arms wouldn't do me any good. My thin sidefins and tailfins allow me to swim through the ocean like a dart through the air. I live in the ocean, but I still need oxygen to live. Luckily, I breathe through gills, not lungs, which filter oxygen from the water. I also have large round eyes that allow me to see better in the ocean. I make my home along a coral reef where there are plenty of places to find food and hide from predators."

Adaptation	How does the adaptation help the animal survive?

"I have four legs that were made for crawling and digging, and that's what I do. I burrow underground to make my home and to find food. I have a narrow, pointed nose and powerful legs for tunneling through the earth. I have very poor eyesight, but that's okay—I have characteristics that are even better for surviving underground. The sensitive hairs on my nose help me feel my way around in the dark. I don't have big ears, but I have great hearing. I can sense the tiniest noise vibrations—like the movement of a tasty worm squirming in the earth."

Adaptation	How does the adaptation help the animal survive?

PART B: Match each bird picture in the diagram to the text that best describes its structural adaptation's uses and benefits.

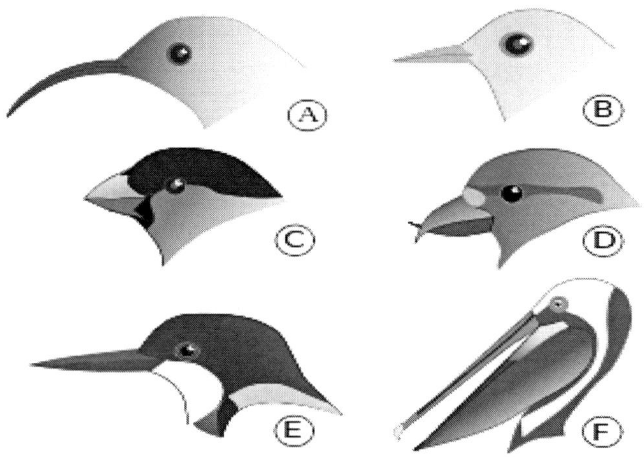

1. ______ *"I use my large beak for scooping large fish out of the ocean and carrying them in a pouch near my throat. I can drain the water from this pouch before swallowing the fish."*
2. ______ *"In England, they call me a red crossbill. My crossed beak helps me pry open the tough layers of pine cones and pull out the seeds."*
3. ______ *"I fly above the water until I spy a fish. I dart just a little into the water and spear my prey with my long, straight, sharp beak."*
4. ______ *"I sip delicious nectar from inside flowers. My long, slender beak is especially useful for getting into those hard to reach places."*
5. ______ *"Insects are very small and hard to catch. That's why my beak is short and sharp for catching and holding insects. My beak is also thin for poking around in old tree trunks where spiders and small insects hide."*
6. ______ *"Most grains are protected by a shell. Luckily, I have a wide, stubby, powerful beak for cracking and smashing grain so I can eat it."*

PART C: Answer the questions below.

1. What is the common purpose of all these beak adaptations? Explain.
2. Most birds can fly. Use what you know and make inferences to explain how the ability to fly helps birds in each of these ways:
   A. Finding Food B. Protection C. Migration

Living Together

Read the text and table. Then answer the questions.

A habitat is the area where plants and animals naturally live. Within a habitat, there are many different kinds of living things. A population is a group of the same kind of living thing, living in the same place at the same time. For example, if 20 fish live in a pond, and 12 are goldfish, the pond has a population of 12 goldfish.

In any habitat, resources such as water, nutrients, and food are limited. Therefore, plant and animal populations must often compete with one another for the resources they need. A habitat cannot support unlimited populations of plants and animals.

The variety of plants, animals, and other organisms, along with nonliving elements like water, soil, sunlight, and climate, in a habitat form an ecosystem. Everything within an ecosystem is connected, and changes can upset the balance of life.

Key Factors that Limit Population			
For Plants		**For Animals**	
a	Competition for nutrients	Competition for food	g
b	Competition for water	Competition for water	h
c	Competition for space	Competition for space	i
d	Competition for sunlight	Disease	j
e	Disease	Predators	k
f	Grazing animals		

1. Write the word from the text that best completes each sentence:
   A. The pond plus the plants and animals living in and around the pond are all part of a/an ___________ .
   B. A bird caught 2 goldfish from the pond. The __________ of goldfish in the pond decreased from 12 goldfish to 10 goldfish.
   C. The goldfish share their __________ with other fish and plant-life.

2. What factor(s) affecting population are described in each example?
   A. ___ Lily pads have wide leaves that float on the surface of the water, blocking sunlight to underwater plants.
   B. ___ The goldfish population has grown as big as it can, based on the size of the pond and what the plant life in the pond can support.
   C. ___ A turtle crawled into the pond and ate one of the goldfish.
   D. ___ The edge of the pond is overgrown with ferns and cattails.

READING INFORMATIONAL TEXT

The Grays Are Coming!

Read the text and answer the questions.

The red squirrel was once a common sight in the forests of the United Kingdom. It lived there abundantly, in its natural habitat, eating seeds and nuts from the trees.

In 1876, an English banker named Thomas Brocklehurst traveled to the United States. He was intrigued by the gray squirrels he saw in the U.S., since they were different than the red squirrels he was used to, so he took two of them with him when he returned home to the U.K. Thinking the gray squirrels harmless, Brocklehurst released them to live in his garden. Soon, other English gentlemen decided to add gray squirrels to their gardens, too.

In just a few years, the population of gray squirrels exploded, as they rapidly reproduced, growing and growing in number. The gray squirrels soon invaded the forest habitats of the red squirrels.

The large population of gray squirrels ate many of the seeds and nuts normally eaten by the red squirrels. Gray squirrels also ate tree bark, which eventually kills trees, destroying the red squirrels' natural habitat and future food supply. To make matters worse, the gray squirrels brought pox disease that killed much of the red squirrel population in the United Kingdom.

Today, the red squirrel can only be found in a few forests in the United Kingdom. Gray squirrels are now the common sight.

1. "Foreshadowing" is a literary device by which a future event is indicated beforehand. Which sentence in the text foreshadows the red squirrel population decrease?
2. An "invasive species" is usually defined as <u>a non-native species</u>[1] that <u>grows its population</u>[2] and <u>harms the habitat it invades</u>[3]. Cite evidence from the text to explain how the gray squirrel meets all three parts.
3. Create a graphic organizer that shows the chain of events of how two gray squirrels wiped out almost an entire population of red squirrels.
4. What can you infer about the natural habitat of gray squirrels? Explain your reasoning.
5. Research an invasive species and create a short report for your class.

COMPARE & CONTRAST

Biomes

Read the text and answer the questions.

A biome is a large region or community that includes plants and animals that have similar environmental needs. A biome is similar to a habitat, but bigger. A biome includes the physical environment (including landforms, climate, soil, natural resources) as well as the plants, animals, and other organisms that live there.

There is not one universally accepted official list of biomes, because not all scientists classify biomes the same way. Some scientists use <u>broad</u> definitions of biomes and they may list as few as 5 or 6 different types of biomes. Some scientists use more <u>narrow</u> definitions, and as a result, they may divide the earth into dozens of different biomes. In either case, biomes may be divided into smaller categories based on even more specific details. Latitude, humidity/rainfall, and elevation are factors that affect how biomes are categorized. Plant structures, leaf type, and plant spacing/density are used too.

Terrestrial (land) biomes are typically defined by their climate and dominant vegetation. Global terrestrial biomes can include grassland, tundra, desert, tropical rainforest, and deciduous and coniferous forests. Aquatic (water) biomes are often defined as freshwater and marine.

1. *A habitat is the environment where an animal or plant naturally lives.* Use words and graphics/illustrations to explain how a habitat and biome are similar and how they are different.
2. What is the main difference between a terrestrial biome and an aquatic biome?
3. Use the text to explain the difference between a <u>broad</u> definition and <u>narrow</u> definition.
4. List at least 5 factors that are commonly used to categorize biomes.
5. A. Make inferences based on the text to describe at least three similarities that animals in the same biome are likely to share.
   B. Make inferences to describe at least three similarities that plants in the same biome are likely to share. Explain your reasoning.

Nonliving Factors

Read the text and answer the questions.

Habitats are affected by physical characteristics like climate, soil, water, and landforms. These nonliving factors have a big impact on the plants and animals that live there.

Climate is the weather in an area over a long period of time. Rainfall and temperature are two features of climate that greatly affect what plants and animals can live in a particular habitat. For example, tropical plants cannot grow in the desert because they need heavy rainfall. Similarly, a polar bear is suited to living in an arctic climate, but alligators are not.

Soil is the loose top layer of the earth's surface. It is made up of broken-down rocks, minerals, and organic material. It provides minerals and nutrients that are essential to life. Different types of plants grow in different types of soil. Fertile soil is full of water and minerals, so it can support many types of plants. Loose, rocky soil is home for many types of trees. Fine silt is often home to grasses.

All habitats include water, because plants and animals cannot live without water. A habitat may include lots of rainfall or just a little. This affects the types and quantity of plants and animals that live there. A source of water like a lake or river or ocean can be an essential part of a habitat for many plants and animals.

Landforms, such as mountains and plains, create conditions that may be ideal for some plants and animals, but unsuitable for others. For example, mountain goats are able to keep their footing on the sides of steep mountains whereas most animals cannot.

1. A. Summarize the main idea of the text.
   B. Describe how the main idea is developed and supported.
   C. Create a graphic organizer to summarize the important ideas in the text.

2. "Unfriendly" habitats have harsh conditions such as little water or extreme temperatures, but plants and animals still live there. Use the text and logical thinking to make inferences about the following:
   A. Characteristics of plants and animals in unfriendly habitats
   B. Quantity of plants and animals in unfriendly habitats
   C. Benefits to plants and animals from living in an unfriendly habitat

Habitats Report

Work with a partner or group to complete one of the habitat research & presentation projects. After the presentations, answer the discussion questions as a class.

Temperate Forest

There are two types of temperate forests—deciduous and coniferous. Deciduous trees have leaves. Coniferous trees have needles.

In the winter, there is less water available for trees' roots to absorb, so trees need to store and use less water. Deciduous trees lose water through their leaves, so they drop their leaves in winter. Coniferous trees only lose a little water through their needles, so they do not drop their needles in the winter, earning them the nickname "evergreens."

Using the materials listed, design an experiment to demonstrate that coniferous trees lose less water through their needles than deciduous trees lose through their leaves. Write a hypothesis. Record your observations.

Presentation: Explain your experiment design and report your conclusions.

Materials: 2 cups or glasses, filled with water 2 plastic bags
1 twig from a coniferous tree 1 twig from a deciduous tree

Arctic Tundra and Antarctic Tundra

Use an online resource to research the Arctic tundra and Antarctic tundra. Describe the location, physical characteristics, and climate of each. List at least 2 plants and 2 animals found in the Arctic tundra and 2 plants and 2 animals found in the Antarctic tundra. Explain how each is adapted to the harsh climate.

Presentation: Create a visual display or graphic organizer, comparing and contrasting the Arctic tundra and Antarctic tundra. Include location, climate, physical characteristics, and types of plants and animals. Be creative!

Desert

Every year, the Sahara desert grows in size, covering more and more area. Use an online resource to define and research desertification. List at least 3-5 causes of desertification in Africa. Explain the effects of desertification, and identify possible solutions to prevent the spread of the Sahara desert.

Create a visual poster or a digital presentation to explain the causes, effects, and possible solutions of desertification.

Tropical Rainforest

Tropical rainforests are often called the lungs of the Earth because they absorb carbon dioxide and produce oxygen. They help stabilize the Earth's climate, they are an important part of the Earth's water cycle, they are home to many species of plants and animals, they provide resources used for food and medicine, and they are a popular place to visit. However, rainforests are at risk!

Use online resources to show where the Earth's rainforests are located, and identify at least 5 reasons they are disappearing. For each reason, explain what resource humans are "taking" and why.

Presentation: Create a digital presentation to share your research. Include photographs that illustrate the changes that are occurring to the rainforests.

Grasslands

The wide African savannah has few places to hide, so animals living there tend to be fast runners. Use an online resource to list 5-10 animals found on the African savannah, and 5-10 animals found in other habitats. Find out the maximum speed of each animal, and approximately how far it can run at a fast speed. Create a table or chart comparing the speeds of various animals. List the animals from fastest to slowest. Color-code animals based on their habitat.

Presentation: Use your chart to show your research. Explain the significance of animal speed on the African savannah using your chart as supporting evidence.

Discussion Questions:

1. Temperate forests contain many different types of trees. What kinds of animals and insects include these trees as part of their habitats?
2. What are common misconceptions about the North and South Pole? Discuss what you learned that you didn't know before.
3. Considering the causes of desertification, do you think that any areas of the United States are in danger of desertification? Why or why not?
4. In your opinion, is there a way to preserve the rainforest without depriving people of the products that are made from rainforest resources? Support your opinion with logical reasoning.
5. Compare the speed of animals on the African savannah to the speed of the fastest human being. Is the African savannah a good habitat for a human? Why or why not?

Plant Adaptations

Read the table and answer the questions.

Desert	Grassland	Tropical Rainforest
•Few plants can survive. •Some plants store water in their stems or leaves. •Some plants have a waxy coating on stems and leaves to reduce water loss. •Some plants have leaves with "hair" that helps block sunlight. •Some plants have sharp spines to discourage predators from eating the plant for water. •Many plant roots spread far across the ground to collect any rainwater.	•Many plants have roots that can sprout new plants after a grass fire. •Most trees have thick bark that resists fire. •Roots of prairie grasses extend deep into the ground to absorb as much moisture as possible. •Many grasses spread their seeds with the wind. •Strong root systems prevent animals from pulling prairie plants out of the ground.	•Some plants climb on other plants to reach the sunlight. •Some plants grow on other plants to reach the sunlight. •Many plants have shallow roots to help capture nutrients from the top level of soil. •Waxy leaves and thin, smooth bark cause water to run off and prevent mold growth. •Flowers on the forest floor are designed to lure animals since there is almost no wind on the forest floor to aid in pollination.
Temperate Forest	**Tundra**	**Wetland**
•Many trees are deciduous, meaning they drop their leaves in fall and grow new ones in spring. •Many trees have broad, light leaves to collect lots of sunlight to make food for winter. •In winter, deciduous trees drop their leaves to avoid unnecessary water loss. •Wildflowers grow on the forest floor in spring, before summer tree leaves shade the ground. •Trees have thick bark to protect against cold winters.	•Few plants live here. •Plants are usually short and close to ground to protect from freezing in the long, cold winters. •Plants have shallow roots because roots cannot penetrate the icy ground. •Plants are often dark in color to better absorb heat from sunlight. •Some plants grow in clumps to help protect one another from wind and cold. •Plants remain small because they cannot get large amounts of nutrients from the frozen ground.	•Underwater leaves and stems are flexible to move with water currents. •Some plant stems have air spaces to help them float in changing tides. •Some plant stems have leaves that float on the water's surface to receive sunlight. •Most plants do not have roots. In plants with roots, the roots cling to surfaces but do not collect nutrients. •Most water plants absorb nutrients through their leaves.

1. How have grassland plants adapted to frequent grass fires?
2. List three ways that the changing seasons affect a temperate forest.
3. A. Which two biomes have the most extreme temperatures?
   B. List at least five ways plants adapt to different temperatures.
4. A. Which biome has the least water? Which biome has the most?
   B. List at least five ways plants adapt to different amounts of water.
5. A. What is the primary function of roots in most plants?
   B. What is the primary function of leaves in most plants?
6. A. Explain how animals are both harmful and beneficial to plants.
   B. Infer how plant life is beneficial to animals.

INTERPRETING VISUAL DATA

Biomes and Climate

Look at the graph and answer the questions.

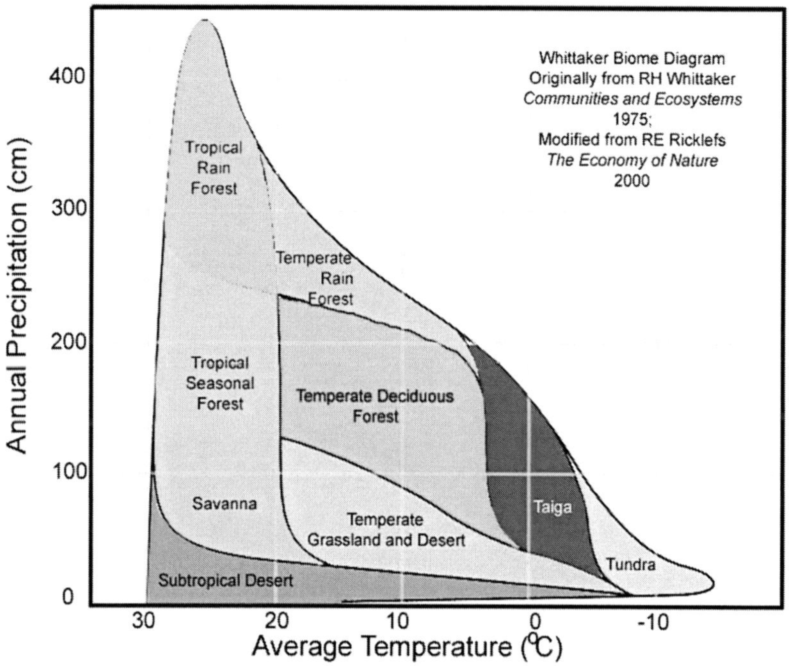

Courtesy of the United States Department of Agriculture

1. Use the graph to identify each biome being described:
   A. Very cold and very dry
   B. Very hot and very rainy
   C. Very hot and very dry
2. How are tropical rainforests and temperate rainforests similar?
3. How does a tiaga differ from tundra?
4. Which definition of <u>temperate</u> best matches the meaning in the graph?
   a) moderate or self-restrained in manner
   b) not subject to long periods of extreme hot or extreme cold
   c) not having an extreme opinion
5. The word "tropical" is typically used to describe the area of land and water surrounding the earth's equator. What can you conclude about the temperature of habitats near the equator? Explain.

Rainforest Habitats

Read the texts and answer the questions.

Rainforests usually have four distinct layers. The habitats of plants and animals are very different from one layer to the next.

October 16: Our Trip to the Amazon Rainforest

It was so hot and humid on the forest floor that sweat trickled down my face. Only 2% of sunlight comes through the forest canopy, so the forest floor was dark. Small ground plants that are suited to little sunlight grow here, as well as moss and mushrooms. I stepped carefully. You never know what might be hiding under the leaves and fallen logs—hairy tarantulas, beetles and other insects, or even slithering anacondas. Our guide told us that large mammals like gorillas and anteaters live on the forest floor, too.

Then, we climbed a rope ladder up into the forest's understory. The understory is above the ground, but below the trees' canopy. Small trees and shrubs here catch the 2-15% of sunlight that shines through. The understory is a dim place where most of the insects live. I saw several types of snakes living here, as well as bright green and orange tree frogs! Luckily, we didn't see any jaguars that like to climb into the understory—yikes!

We climbed higher to reach the forest's canopy, a thick covering of branches and leaves near the top of the rainforest. Breezes from above cooled the canopy and made the air a little less humid. High in the branches, vines and many other air plants (plants that don't need soil) grow. The trees' branches and leaves are so close together they absorb approximately 80% of the sunlight. Animals like monkeys and sloths can travel from branch to branch for more than 60 miles without touching the ground!

Climbing to the very tops of the tallest trees, we reached the emergent layer. This habitat contains only the tallest parts of the tallest trees. It was very sunny at the top. I could hear small monkeys calling from tree to tree. Butterflies and other small insects buzzed about and different types of birds chirped cheerily. Our guide told us that bats come out at night to eat the insects.

1. What does the name “rainforest” tell you about this biome?
2. Complete the graphic organizer by identifying the four layers of the rainforest and the plants and animals that are found in each layer.

<table>
<tr><th>Rainforest layers</th><td rowspan="5">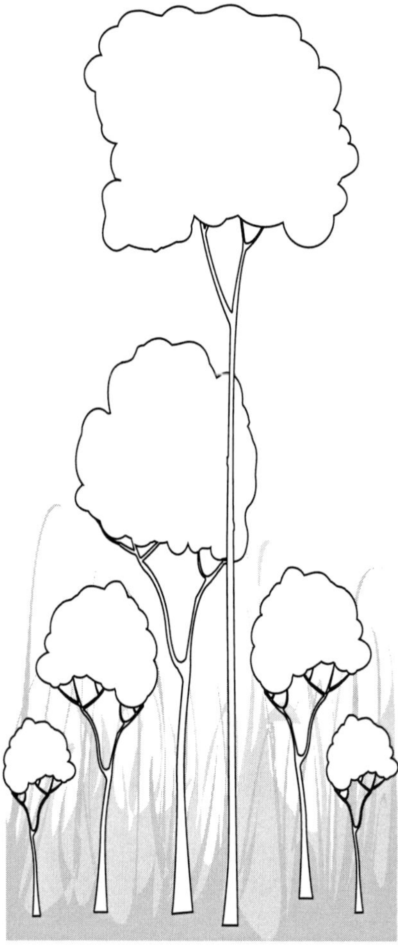</td><th>Animals in each layer</th></tr>
<tr><td></td><td></td></tr>
<tr><td></td><td></td></tr>
<tr><td></td><td></td></tr>
<tr><td></td><td></td></tr>
</table>

3. Why do the bottom layers only receive a limited amount of sunlight?
4. A. Explain how the amount of sunlight affects the types of plants that are found in each layer.
   B. Explain how the amount of sunlight affects the types of plants that are found in each layer.
5. Use the text and make inferences to list at least three factors that cause rainforest habitats to vary from one layer to the next.

The Oceans Are Alive

Read the text and answer the questions.

The ocean is huge! It covers 75% of the surface of the Earth. The ocean is not just one single habitat—it contains many different habitats. Scientists often divide the ocean into different zones. The number of zones varies, as zones can be divided into smaller zones. Habitats within each zone have some common characteristics.

The intertidal zone is the area of water and land between high tide and low tide. This zone gets lots of sunlight and is teeming with life. It is a perfect habitat for sea grasses and algae. Some animals, like barnacles and sea stars, survive the strong ocean tides by attaching themselves to rocks and other sturdy structures.

Extending from the shore to the ocean depths is the pelagic zone. It can be divided into three levels—the euphotic, dysphotic, and aphotic zones.

The euphotic zone is the area from the ocean's surface to about 200 meters (660 feet) below. Because this zone has the most sunlight, it is called the "sunlit zone." It contains over 90% of all marine life, including coral reefs, all marine plant life, and many other animals like whales, porpoises, sharks, jellyfish, and more.

The dysphotic zone, or "twilight zone," is the area from 200 meters (660 feet) to about 1000 meters (3300 feet) below the surface. It is much darker and colder than the euphotic zone. No plants grow in this zone because of lack of light, so most animals in this zone eat other animals. Some animals here swim up or down to a different zone to find food, and some animals feed on plant and animal remains that drift into this zone. Animals in this zone, like squid and hatchet fish, often have muted colors to hide from predators, some have large eyes to see in the dark, and some can even produce their own light!

The aphotic zone, or "midnight zone," is the deepest, darkest part of the ocean, including the ocean floor. It starts at about 1000 meters (3300 feet) and goes down to the bottom of the ocean. No plants and few animals live in this zone. The animals here survive by eating the remains of plants and animals that drift down from the zones above. Anglerfish, sea spiders, and sea cucumbers are some of the few animals that call this zone home.

1. What is the main characteristic used to divide the ocean into zones?
2. Use the text to create a diagram that shows the intertidal zone, the pelagic zone, and the three zones within the pelagic zone.
3. Use a Venn diagram to compare and contrast the three parts of the pelagic zone.

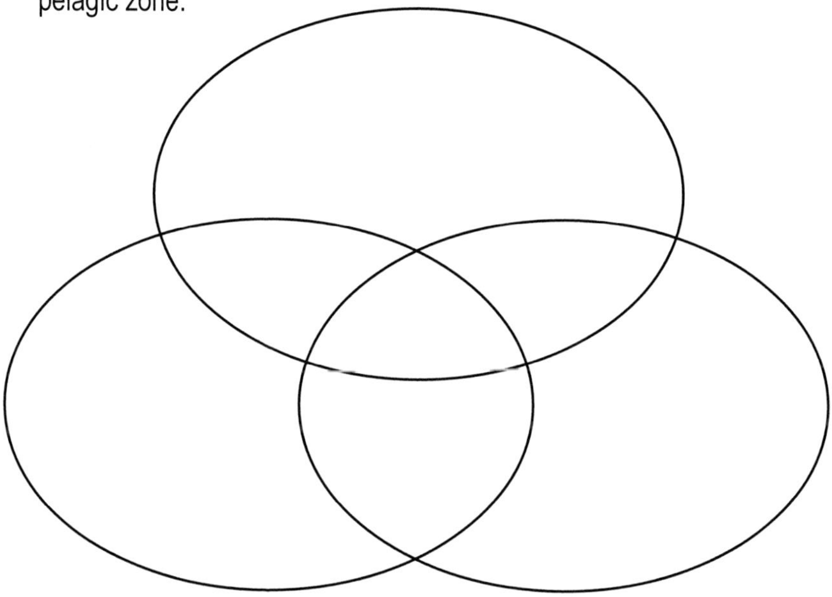

4. Read each statement and identify the zone where the creature lives:
   A. _______________ "I have strong suction cups on my tentacles that help me cling to rocks in the rolling tides."
   B. _______________ "Being able to create my own light helps me see in the dark and keeps me from bumping into hatchet fish."
   C. _______________ "Some people call me a bottom-dweller because I make my home on the cold, sunless ocean floor."
   D. _______________ "I live in the pelagic zone that is the warmest, and that is most affected by weather on the ocean's surface."
   E. _______________ "I live in the water…wait, I live on the land…wait, in the water…wait, on the land!"
5. Explain the meaning of each phrase:
   A. "sunlit zone" B. "twilight zone" C. "midnight zone"
6. Use the text, plus what you know about plants, to explain why the dysphotic and twilight zones are not suitable habitats for plants.

MAP ACTIVITY

Habitat in Crisis!

Answer the questions as described in Part A and Part B.

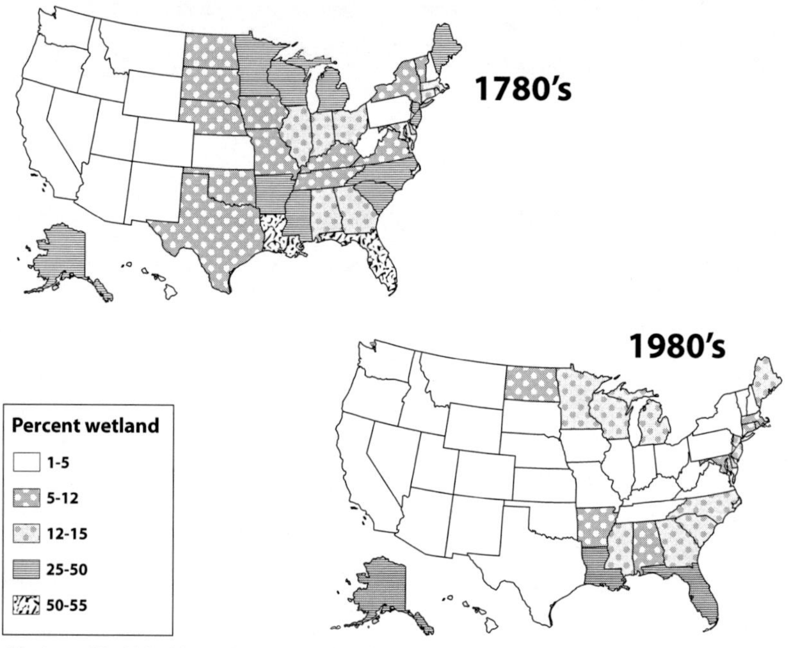

Courtesy of the United States Department of Agriculture: Forest Service

PART A: Use the maps to answer the questions.

1. A. Who created these maps?
   B. What data was used to create the maps?
   C. Why are two maps shown?
   D. Why is only one map key shown?
   E. What is the purpose of the maps?
2. Write an appropriate title to go at the top of the maps.
3. Compare and analyze the maps:
   A. How are they the same?
   B. How are they different?
   C. In what way do the differences on the maps indicate a pattern?
4. Make a prediction about the percentage of wetlands in the United States in 2080. Cite evidence from the maps to support your prediction.

PART B: Read the letter and answer the questions.

1) Dear State Senator,

2) The Senate is voting tomorrow on whether or not to drain the wetlands in our area and develop them into farmland. I understand that farmland is important, but the wetlands are important too!

3) Many plants, fish, amphibians, reptiles, and mammals, depend on our wetlands. If you drain the wetlands, you will destroy their natural habitat! Also, our wetlands are a nursery for hundreds of species of birds that fly to the wetlands to lay and hatch their eggs. Habitat loss could cause some of these birds to become endangered—or maybe even extinct!

4) As important as it is to preserve the habitat of our plants and animals, there are more reasons not to drain the wetlands. Did you know that wetlands help remove toxic chemicals and pollution from our water and air? It's no wonder wetlands are known as the sponges of life! Also, did you know that wetlands prevent flooding by absorbing extra water from too much rain? Imagine the houses and roads that would be flooded if not for our wetlands!

5) With all this information, I hope that you agree that we must save the wetlands! I urge you to vote against allowing our wetlands to be drained.

6) Sincerely,
A concerned citizen

5. A. What is the purpose of the letter?
   B. Is the purpose stated outright or implied? Explain.
   C. How does the author attempt to achieve his or her purpose?
   D. In your opinion is the author effective? Why or why not?

6. Describe the organizational style of the letter by explaining the purpose of each section of the letter, 1-6.

7. Choose the word from each pair that **best** describes the style of the text. Cite examples from the text to explain your choices.
   A. formal *–or–* informal
   B. informative *–or–* narrative
   C. fact *–or–* opinion

8. A. Write an extra paragraph that could be included in the letter, using some of the information from the maps. In your paragraph, cite the source of your information and at least two facts that you got from analyzing the maps.
   B. Does the extra paragraph you wrote make the letter more or less effective? Explain why.

PRIMARY SOURCE ANALYSIS

Political Cartoon

Look at the political cartoon and answer the questions.

The cartoon was created by Herbert Block in 1973.

1. A. What do you notice first in the cartoon? Why?
   B. List 5 additional observations.
2. A. Describe the types of pollution shown in the cartoon.
   B. List 5 causes of pollution that are shown.
3. A. Describe the people shown in the cartoon.
   B. If they were to speak, what do you think they would say? Why?
4. A. Find and describe any animals shown in the cartoon.
   B. If they could speak, what do you think they would say? Why?
5. A. Describe the purpose/objective of the cartoon.
   B. In your opinion, is the cartoon effective? Why or why not?

Conservation Vocabulary

Read the text and complete the vocabulary activity.

Plant and animal habitats are delicate and can be easily destroyed. Some habitat loss is natural, but most is caused by human activities. The actions that occur in one place can negatively affect animals, plants, and humans in other places in the world!

However, people can make positive differences too. As an informed, active citizen, you can consider the effect on habitats when you make personal buying and lifestyle choices; you can affect your community's choices by voting or participating in government; you can volunteer for habitat-helping causes; and you can directly or indirectly help habitats through your future career!

1. Complete the graphic organizer for each word or phrase.

conservation	pesticides	deforestation	pollution
environmentalism	preservation	over-population	recycling
littering	sustainability	emissions	wastefulness

DEFINITION	FACTS/CHARACTERISTICS

WORD

HOW IT RELATES TO HABITATS

2. Classify each vocabulary word as either a **PROBLEM** that contributes to habitat loss, or as a **SOLUTION** that can help avoid or reduce habitat loss, and write it in the correct column on the table below.

PROBLEMS	SOLUTIONS

Correlations to Common Core State Standards

For your convenience, correlations are listed page-by-page, and for the entire book!

This book is correlated to the Common Core State Standards for English Language Arts grades 3-8, and to Common Core State Standards for Literacy in History, Science, & Technological Subjects grades 6-8.

Correlations are highlighted in gray.

PAGE #	READING *Includes:* RI: Reading Informational Text RST: Reading Science & Technical Subjects	WRITING *Includes:* W: Writing WHST: Writing History/Social Studies, Science, & Technical Subjects	LANGUAGE *Includes:* L: Language LF: Language Foundational Skills	SPEAKING & LISTENING *Includes:* SL: Speaking & Listening
2	RI/RST . **1 2 3 4 5** 6 7 **8** 9 **10**	W/WHST . **1 2** 3 **4 5** 6 7 **8 9 10**	L/LF . 1 2 3 **4 5 6**	SL . 1 2 3 4 5 6
3	RI/RST . **1 2 3 4 5** 6 7 **8** 9 **10**	W/WHST . 1 **2** 3 **4** 5 6 7 **8 9 10**	L/LF . 1 2 3 **4 5 6**	SL . 1 2 3 4 5 6
4-5	RI/RST . **1** 2 **3 4 5** 6 7 **8** 9 **10**	W/WHST . **1 2 3 4 5** 6 7 **8 9 10**	L/LF . 1 2 **3 4** 5 **6**	SL . 1 2 3 4 5 6
6-7	RI/RST . **1 2 3 4 5 6 7 8 9 10**	W/WHST . 1 **2** 3 **4** 5 6 7 **8 9 10**	L/LF . 1 2 3 **4** 5 **6**	SL . 1 2 3 4 5 6
8	RI/RST . **1** 2 **3 4 5** 6 **7** 8 **9 10**	W/WHST . 1 2 3 4 5 6 7 **8** 9 **10**	L/LF . 1 2 3 **4** 5 **6**	SL . 1 2 3 4 5 6
9	RI/RST . **1** 2 **3 4 5** 6 7 **8 9 10**	W/WHST . 1 **2 3 4 5 6 7** 8 9 **10**	L/LF . 1 2 3 **4 5 6**	SL . **1** 2 3 **4** 5 **6**
10	RI/RST . **1 2 3 4 5** 6 7 **8** 9 **10**	W/WHST . 1 **2** 3 **4** 5 6 7 8 **9 10**	L/LF . 1 2 3 **4 5 6**	SL . 1 2 3 4 5 6
11	RI/RST . **1 2 3** 4 **5** 6 7 **8** 9 **10**	W/WHST . 1 **2** 3 **4** 5 6 7 8 **9 10**	L/LF . 1 2 3 4 5 6	SL . 1 2 3 4 5 6
12-13	RI/RST . **1 2** 3 4 5 6 **7** 8 **9 10**	W/WHST . **1 2** 3 **4 5 6 7 8 9 10**	L/LF . 1 2 **3 4** 5 **6**	SL . **1 2** 3 **4 5 6**
14	RI/RST . **1** 2 **3** 4 **5** 6 **7** 8 **9 10**	W/WHST . 1 **2** 3 4 5 6 7 **8 9 10**	L/LF . 1 2 3 4 5 6	SL . 1 2 3 4 5 6
15	RI/RST . **1 2 3 4 5** 6 **7 8** 9 **10**	W/WHST . 1 **2** 3 **4** 5 6 7 **8** 9 **10**	L/LF . 1 2 3 **4** 5 **6**	SL . 1 2 3 4 5 6
16-17	RI/RST . **1** 2 **3 4 5** 6 7 **8** 9 **10**	W/WHST . 1 **2** 3 **4** 5 6 7 **8** 9 **10**	L/LF . 1 2 3 **4 5 6**	SL . 1 2 3 4 5 6
18-19	RI/RST . **1 2 3** 4 **5** 6 7 **8** 9 **10**	W/WHST . 1 **2** 3 **4** 5 6 7 **8 9 10**	L/LF . 1 2 3 **4** 5 **6**	SL . 1 2 3 4 5 6
20-21	RI/RST . **1 2 3 4 5 6 7 8 9 10**	W/WHST . **1 2 3 4 5** 6 7 **8 9 10**	L/LF . 1 2 3 **4** 5 **6**	SL . 1 2 3 4 5 6
22	RI/RST . **1 2** 3 4 **5 6 7 8** 9 **10**	W/WHST . 1 **2** 3 **4** 5 6 7 8 **9 10**	L/LF . 1 2 3 4 5 6	SL . 1 2 3 4 5 6
23	RI/RST . 1 2 3 **4** 5 6 7 8 **9 10**	W/WHST . 1 2 3 4 5 6 7 8 9 10	L/LF . 1 2 3 **4** 5 **6**	SL . 1 2 3 4 5 6
COMPLETE BOOK	RI/RST . **1 2 3 4 5 6 7 8 9 10**	W/WHST . **1 2 3 4 5 6 7 8 9 10**	L/LF . 1 2 **3 4 5 6**	SL . **1 2** 3 **4 5 6**

For the complete Common Core standard identifier, combine your grade + "." + letter code above + "." + number code above.

In addition to the correlations indicated here, the activities may be adapted or expanded to align to additional standards and to meet the diverse needs of your unique students!